CW00848298

THE MEMORY DETECTIVES

THE MEMORY DETECTIVES

Julia Amos

illustrated by
Susanna Kendall

CHARLCOMBE BOOKS

Charlcombe Books
17 George's Road, Bath BA1 6EY
Tel 01225-335813

First published 2018

ISBN 978 1 9996558 1 5

Printed and bound in Great Britain by
CPI Antony Rowe, Chippenham, Wilts

CHAPTER 1

Dear Mr Barshot,

We have an elderly resident who arrived at our care home from hospital about six months ago. Her name is Hattie Barshot but we have very little information about her.

Hattie appears to have some memory loss and seems depressed. She has lost touch with her family and has never had any visitors.

We are hoping to trace some family or friends for Hattie and we think that you may be a relative?

CHAPTER 2

Ben pushed open the back door. Mum was working evenings this week, so Grandad would be here to cook supper. He sniffed. Pizza! Excellent! (And Grandad never counted how many slices he had.) Ben threw off his coat and hurried into the kitchen.

'Ah, there you are, lad. Hungry?'

'Starving!'

Grandad was just taking the pizza out of the oven, the cheese bubbling on the top.

'How was school?'

'OK.' Ben fetched two plates from the rack. 'We've got a new girl. Doesn't say much. Maybe her English isn't too good. She's *very* good at drawing, though.'

Grandad waggled his eyebrows. 'Ah, some competition for you, then!'

Ben laughed. 'Yeah, maybe ...' He added another slice of pizza to his plate. 'Oh, and Joe played his clarinet in assembly today. He was brilliant!'

'It's a lovely instrument if it's well played.'

'Yeah, he's getting pretty good. One of his sisters plays the trumpet in the Air Cadets Band. Joe wants to join too, as soon as he's old enough.'

'Ah! A man with a plan! I like that. And is Alex coming round later?'

'No, he's got Science Club tonight.'

'Good for him.'

Grandad leaned back in his chair. 'I hear that you and your mum went to visit Cousin Hattie at the weekend. That was kind of you. I feel bad that I couldn't come too, but with the art exhibition only a couple of weeks away, I'm up to my eyes at the moment, making the display boards.'

Ben nodded briefly and turned away.

'Hattie back in England after all these years and none of us knew. How did it go?'

Ben shrugged. He dug fiercely into his pizza. His grandad studied him a moment then poured himself a cup of tea and picked up the newspaper. The fridge hummed and there was an occasional rustle as Grandad turned a page.

Ben suddenly burst out, 'It was awful. She didn't understand who we were, though Mum tried to explain, and then Mum tried to hold her hand and talk to her but she just turned her head away and didn't say anything. So we just sat there. For ages! AND Mum was all snappy with me in the car coming back. It's not fair. It's not my fault Hattie was so BORING.'

'Oh dear, well, she must be very old now, I suppose, in her nineties, in fact, but from what I was told, she was a bit of a tearaway. The family never knew what she'd be up to next! I've been searching the family photo albums and I've found a photo of her. I brought it over. I'll show you.'

Grandad dug around in a carrier bag and produced an old leather photo album, brown and rather tatty. He searched through. 'Look, that's her, on the farm where they lived. She's driving the tractor.'

'That's Hattie?'

'Yes, that's definitely her.'

The faded black and white photo had creases and brown patches but it showed a young woman, waving confidently as she drove an old-fashioned tractor up a field.

'It's a nice picture, isn't it?' said Grandad. 'But what's really surprising is what it says on the back.'

The writing was faint and spidery but Ben could just make it out:

'Hattie, 1938, taken the day she repaired the Fordson's engine!'

Ben looked at the photo again. He tried to imagine Hattie as this laughing girl on the tractor, a girl who could fix an engine. He tried but couldn't do it.

Grandad closed the album. 'That's the only photo I've got of her, I'm afraid. I never met her. During the war, she probably stayed on at the farm as part of the Women's Land Army.

'Women's Land Army?'

'Women who worked on the farms while the men were at war. Perhaps you could ask her next time you go.'

'I'm not going back. There's no point! I don't know if she understands anything, and she certainly doesn't want to talk to *us*.'

'Maybe she doesn't like questions.' Grandad thought for a minute. 'Perhaps if you took something to show her, something she might recognise, then she might open up?'

Ben shrugged.

'I tell you what, if I lend you the photo, could you print it out much bigger, and maybe find some pictures of Land Army girls too?'

'The printer's on the blink.'

'Well, at school then?'

'I suppose …'

'It might just spark some memories. Just give it one more go. Please. I'm not promising anything but you never know …'

CHAPTER 3

'Miss, can I use the photocopier, please? I want to print this photo out much bigger.'

'Is it for school work, Ben?'

'Well, no …' And Ben explained.

'So, she might have been in the Land Army? Well, we could count that as a local history topic, I suppose. All right, yes, and then you can tell the class what you discover.' And she moved away before Ben could think of any excuse.

Someone chuckled behind him and Ben swung round. He didn't know anyone had been listening. It was Alex.

'Don't worry. She'll probably have forgotten all about it by next week. Hey, let's have a look.' He bent over the little picture.

'Ah, yes, she's on a Fordson.'

'What?'

'The tractor. It's a Fordson.'

'How on earth do you know that!'

'Models. I do much more complicated kits now, of course, but I started with little ones. I remember doing the Fordson tractor. That was one of my first.'

He straightened up. 'Do you think she would like to see it?'

***

When Ben, his mum and Alex came into Hattie's room, she looked past them into the corridor.

'Where's Thomas?' she asked. 'I want Thomas. I keep telling them, but they won't fetch him.'

Ben looked at his mum but it seemed that she too didn't know what to say. She put her hand on Hattie's arm. 'Who's Thomas, Hattie?' she asked, gently.

Hattie shook her off. 'My brother, of course,' she replied crossly. 'And I don't know who you all are, so you can just go away!'

Ben and Alex started to back towards the door but Ben's mum shook her head. 'We will go away in a minute, Hattie, if that's what you want, but first will you have a look at the photo Ben has brought you?' And she beckoned Ben over.

Ben edged closer, holding the enlarged photo out in front of him like a shield. Hattie glanced towards him and then at the photo. Her expression changed. She reached for the photo and studied it carefully. 'I think I know that tractor and that farm gate.'

'That's you on the tractor, Hattie,' ventured Ben. 'It says so on the back.'

'Is it? Yes, perhaps it is. I liked driving tractors.'

Then Ben showed her a picture of a group of laughing girls, wearing green shirts and khaki dungarees and holding pitchforks. Hattie glanced at it. 'Land Army girls. We had some of them on the farm.'

Alex carefully placed his model tractor on the table next to Hattie. Hattie put her head on one side. She scrutinised the model closely, then she looked up. 'You made a good job of that.'

Alex blushed. 'Well … thanks. I used too much glue ... see, there, and on there ... and it took me ages, but it was my first kit. I'm quicker now. Look, this is a better one.' And he placed a model of a little plane on the table.

Hattie reached for it immediately. 'Oh, a little Tiger Moth!' She ran her finger gently all over the plane. 'Cockpit … wings … tail … Yes, that's it,' she murmured. 'Funny little planes, Tiger Moths.' Suddenly she laughed. 'Freezing cold in the winter in that open cockpit. I sometimes took a hot water bottle up with me!'

CHAPTER 4

Miss Walker did not forget. 'Ben has been to visit someone who may have been a Land Army girl in the war,' she told the class. 'How did you get on with the photo, Ben?'

Ben blushed. Everyone was looking at him so he had to say something.

'Um, well, she says she *wasn't* in the Land Army … but she is a bit confused. She says', he paused, doubtfully, 'she *says* that she flew planes …'

Joe's hand shot up.

'Miss, Miss, she can't have done. The Air Force didn't have women pilots in the Second World War. Only men.' He gave Ben an apologetic shrug.

'Ah … a mystery, then,' said Miss Walker. 'Well, we'll have to leave that for now but perhaps it is something for you to investigate, Ben?' And she turned to the rest of the class. 'We're going to be doing some more online research. You can work in pairs ...'

Ben was disappointed. Joe knew a lot about the Air Force. If he said Hattie couldn't have flown planes then he was probably right.

Alex, though, head forward, was rapidly searching through sites online. He nudged Ben. 'Look,' he whispered, 'I've found some photos of World War II women pilots.'

'So she *could* have flown planes!'

'Looks like it. Yes. Says here ...' Miss Walker turned and gave them a long, suspicious look. 'Show you later.'

***

Joe was not easily convinced. 'There are lots of Second World War photos in the hut where the band rehearses. I've been there with my sister. There are *no* women pilots.'

But Alex started to show him the online photos. No doubt about it, some of the pilots were female.

Ben read the caption '*Women ferry pilots, Second World War.*'

'What does *ferry pilot* mean, Joe?'

Joe shrugged. 'No idea. Something to do with the Navy?' he suggested, doubtfully.

To their surprise, the new girl, Milena, leaned over

to join in the conversation. 'In war against Nazis, they have woman pilots. I know this. Old lady in my village, dead now, she say she is pilot.'

'In Poland, you mean?' asked Ben.

Milena shook her head vigorously.

'She is Polish, yes, but she cannot fly planes in Poland! Germans very quickly come from north, from west, from south, and then Russians coming from other way. She escape and come here, to UK to help.'

This time Joe nodded. 'Yes,' he said slowly, 'there were Polish pilots in our Air Force, lots of them. Their record was pretty amazing. But women pilots …?'

Then Alex found something interesting. 'Got it. Ferry pilots … worked for the *Air Transport Auxiliary*. Not fighter pilots. They delivered planes from one place to another. Listen, *"From aircraft factory to airfield, or from airfield to airfield, wherever a plane was needed in Britain, male and female pilots from the Air Transport Auxiliary flew them there."* '

Suddenly everything began to fall into place. Milena was right, and Hattie too might be telling the truth. They started to search other sites.

'Hey, Ben, I've found an ATA museum and they've got lots more photos of women pilots. Look! Do you think one of them could be Hattie, or the old lady from your village, Milena?'

Ben wasn't listening. He had spotted something else. 'The museum's got a flight simulator. You can have a go at handling all the controls!'

'Which plane?' asked Joe, quickly,

'Says here, it's a Spitfire.'

'A Spitfire!' breathed Alex. 'We have to go! We just *have* to.'

***

Ben's mum pursed her lips. 'It's quite a long way to Maidenhead. A lot of petrol, and we don't even know for certain that Hattie really was a pilot. She might just be remembering what someone else told her …'

'Mum, it's 59.2 miles and would only take us an hour and a quarter if you went on the motorway …'

His mum laughed. 'You *have* been doing your research!'

'Yes, we have. Oh, please, Mum … *please*. It's only a little museum so it isn't expensive … and I'll save up my pocket money.'

'All right, tell you what. If you can prove to me that Hattie *definitely* flew planes for the Air Transport Auxiliary then I'll take you all to the museum at half-term. I'll pay for the flight simulator flights if you and your friends pay your own entrance money. How about that?'

Ben beamed. 'I'll tell the others. I'm sure that will be OK.'

CHAPTER 5

When Ben, Alex and Joe arrived at Hattie's room, the carer had just cleared away her lunch tray.

'Did you enjoy your lunch?' asked Joe politely.

'Oh …' replied Hattie, looking around vaguely, 'I suppose I must have had something … I don't remember what …'

Ben nudged him, 'Joe, have you got the posters?' Joe nodded. He unrolled a large poster of an aircraft and held it in front of Hattie.

'Oh, a Hurricane,' said Hattie at once. 'We had a lot of those.'

The boys exchanged glances. This was a good start. Joe held up another poster.

'Lancaster. She was four-engined, of course, so I wasn't allowed to fly those, but some of the girls did.'

Joe looked startled. 'They flew four-engined planes!'

'Oh yes.'

Then Ben opened up his laptop and did a quick search online. Soon he had found lots more images of Second World War aircraft. Hattie peered forward. 'Douglas,' she proclaimed. 'And that's a Hellcat, I rather enjoyed flying those. Walrus, could be a bit of a brute. Oh yes, a Hudson, I remember them.' She reeled off all the names without any hesitation. The boys looked at one another in amazement.

Then it was Alex's turn. 'I've brought you another model aircraft, Hattie. Thought you'd like this one.'

Hattie's eyes fastened on the little plane. She broke into a huge grin. 'A Spitfire!' she cried, reaching for it. 'A darling aeroplane to fly. It almost seemed to read your mind. You hardly had to touch the joystick to move her around. It would do anything you wanted. I loved flying them. We all did.'

'Would you like to keep it? I can easily make another.' Hattie pressed her hands together in delight.

'Hattie,' asked Joe, 'did you really fly all these different planes?'

'Practically all. We all wanted to fly as many different ones as we could. We kept a tally.' Hattie straightened her back. 'I flew thirty-four different planes!'

'Wow! That's amazing!' exclaimed Joe. 'But how did you do it? They must have had different controls.'

'Well, we had some general training, of course, but then we just relied on the *pilots' notes*.'

'*Pilots' notes*?'

'A little handbook that told us all the important things about each plane.'

'That doesn't sound much to go on!'

'Well no, I suppose it doesn't – but we got pretty good at it. Besides, it was wartime. We read the notes, climbed into the plane and took off.'

And though it scarcely seemed possible, they now no longer doubted her. Somehow they just knew that Hattie was telling the truth.

CHAPTER 6

At the museum, they explained about Hattie. The steward who greeted them was enthusiastic.

'You actually know a former ATA pilot! Well, this is very special. I'll go and fetch our chairman. He's in today. He'll certainly want to talk to you.'

And he did.

'Hattie Barshot. Oh yes, I recognise that name, of course. We've got details of all the ferry pilots here. We keep in touch with all those who are still alive – not many now, sadly. But Hattie, now that *is* interesting. We'd lost touch with her.'

'She was living abroad for many years,' explained Ben's mum.

'Ah ... well, yes. Almost impossible for women pilots to get jobs here after the war. Too many pilots and, I'm sorry to say, a lot of discrimination against women. The men got all the jobs, even if the women had wider experience.'

'That's not right!' exclaimed Joe, loudly.

'It's not, but that's how it was. Now let's get her details up. Here we are ... Hattie, joined in 1942. She did some of her early training at Thame and then later near here at White Waltham.'

'She says she flew nearly *all* the planes …'

'Yes, she would have done. By the end of the war she was first officer rank and cleared to fly all the single and twin-engined planes. But come and have a look over here. This is a photo of some of the women pilots, taken in 1945. There she is, that's Hattie, in the middle there.'

They all stood in front of the photo, amazed. The large black and white image showed a group of female pilots in their uniforms, standing under the wing of an enormous aircraft. Hattie's hair was blowing in the wind and she had her arms around the shoulders of her comrades. She was beaming at the camera. This is who she was. A pilot. And good at it, it seemed.

'I'll print you off a copy, and I'll do some hunting in our archives later, let you know what else I find.'

'That would be very kind,' said Mum.

'Oh, and you mentioned a Polish woman pilot. Pity you don't have her name but she might be in that photo too.' He pointed, 'Both Jadwiga and Stefania there were Polish. We had pilots from many parts of Europe already overrun by the Nazis. Others came from further afield, India, South Africa, Australia and New Zealand, Ethiopia – even one from China.'

'And Americans too, I expect?' suggested Ben's mum.

'Oh yes, we had a lot of help from pilots from the USA and Canada, of course. Hattie would have known some of them. There was one pilot from South America too, from Chile. She was based at Hamble, like Hattie.'

'Were any of the pilots from the Caribbean?' asked Joe.

'Not in the ATA, as it happens, but the RAF certainly had Caribbean pilots.' He smiled, 'Of course, the Air Force had first pick. ATA got the "rejects", the ones a bit too old, or missing part of a limb, or women pilots, of course, or ...'

'Missing part of a limb!' interrupted Ben. 'How on earth could they fly planes?'

'I know. It's incredible. But they did. They were all experienced pilots determined to keep flying. Used their elbows, knees, whatever it took …' He shrugged. 'But I mustn't go on. You three have booked flights in the simulator, haven't you? Ever done this before?'

Joe nodded, 'I have, once before. Not a Spitfire, though. The others haven't.'

'Right, then. Well, your instructor's waiting for you. Who's going first?'

CHAPTER 7

Ben, Alex and Joe burst into Hattie's room.

'We've flown in a Spitfire!' cried Ben.

'Well, just the cockpit, but it had all the controls …' amended Alex.

'And it had screens in front and on each side…' added Joe.

'Yes, big screens, so we could look ahead at the sky, or down on the land, just like in a real aeroplane … It was so cool!'

Hattie looked at them in bewilderment.

'Alex looped over so fast he was nearly sick!'

'No, I wasn't!'

'*And* we had a go at landing her,' added Joe.

'Yes, they gave us extra time because we knew *you*! Joe was best but Alex kangaroo-hopped like anything …'

'What about you, Ben! You zigzagged all over the airfield!'

Hattie started to chuckle.

Joe turned to her. 'The joy stick was really simple to use, Hattie, just like you said it would be. It moved the plane around so easily.'

Hattie was watching him closely now.

'And what was the thing on the left, Joe?' asked Ben.

'The throttle – faster and slower.'

'And then there were the flaps, and the undercarriage thing …'

'That was on the right,' said Alex.

'Oh yes, on the right. But we didn't do that, Hattie. The instructor controlled the undercarriage for us.'

Hattie suddenly smiled. 'Coming into land *is* complicated. Lots of things to remember. But sometimes, in good weather, I didn't *want* to come down. Not really. It's wonderful up there, simply wonderful! Free as a bird. I was based at an airfield near Southampton. I could look down from my plane and see the ships out at sea.'

They looked at her in amazement. Hattie was chatting to them, chatting just like there wasn't anything wrong with her memory at all.

Alex had an idea. 'Looking down … that's a thought. Google Earth, Ben?'

Ben raised an eyebrow, then realised, 'Oh, yes, great idea! Did you say near Southampton, Hattie?'

'Yes, at Hamble. We were all women pilots there.'

Ben moved closer to Hattie, and the other two crowded round. Ben gradually zoomed in. Hattie craned her neck forward in excitement.

'Oh, it's like magic! I never thought … Oh, that's the Isle of Wight to the south, can't miss that, and now we are coming into, into …' Hattie's face changed. She looked bewildered. 'What are all these buildings? Where's the airfield? It should be … Oh, where has it gone? I know it should be …' Her forehead creased with anxiety. She glanced over to the window. The sky was heavily overcast.

'The cloud is very low. They mustn't get stuck above cloud cover or they'll never find their way down. And what if they can't find the airfield to land? … Oh dear …!' She peered at the screen then twisted her head towards the window again. 'Visibility is getting worse, and there are barrage balloons nearby! They are going to get entangled in the wires!' She became more and more distressed and angry. 'They need to get down quickly!' shouted Hattie.

The boys were appalled. They couldn't make sense of what she was saying. What had they done?

One of the carers came in and tried to calm Hattie. 'Best if you go now, boys,' she said, quietly. 'Not your fault. She gets like this sometimes.'

They left, feeling awful. Everything had gone wrong.

CHAPTER 8

Grandad piled extra chips on Ben's plate.

'Don't worry, lad. You weren't to know things had changed, or how she would react. Anyway, it was a good idea. Maybe that bloke at the museum could tell you which airfields *haven't* changed and you could try again. I think she'd like that.'

Ben shuddered. 'I don't think so. I don't even know if she'll ever want to see us again.'

'Of course she'll want to see you. Don't forget, her memory isn't too good. She remembers lots of things from the past really clearly, but chances are she'll have forgotten all about that little incident by the time you next see her.'

***

Outside the care home a man was loading a keyboard and amplifiers into a van.

'Look at that, Ben,' said his mum. 'They must have had an entertainer. That's nice. I wonder if Hattie went down to the lounge to hear him.'

Ben didn't reply.

When they got inside, Mum asked a carer.

'Oh yes, she was there, and she enjoyed it. Tapping her foot, she was, and joining in the songs. She's back in her room now, probably having a rest after all that excitement.'

Having a rest. Good, thought Ben. Maybe she'd be asleep and they could just go home. But as they approached Hattie's room, it was clear that she was *not* having a rest. They could hear loud, husky singing and regular thumps.

'Doo bi, doo bi, doo bi, doo bi, doo bi, Doo-Doo!' sang Hattie.

They peeped in. She paused to wave cheerily to them and then set to again, thwacking the arms of her comfy chair like a drummer. Ben was so relieved that he started to laugh. Hattie didn't seem to mind at all. In fact it seemed to egg her on.

'Doo bi, doo bi, doo bi, doo bi, doo bi, Doo-Doo!' bellowed Hattie.

Mum joined in, clapping the beats but Ben had another idea. They had to have a recording of this! Hattie ended with a little flourish of her hand and grinned at them.

'That's quite a song! Do you know what it's called, Hattie?' asked Mum.

'Can't remember … but I remember the dance bands. They were wonderful during the war. We'd go up to London if we could and dance the night away – get the late train back to base and then up flying in the morning! We had such fun!'

'But weren't you worried about the Blitz?'

'You couldn't worry about bombs all the time! Anyway, Southampton was getting bombed too. No, if it happened, it happened. We were young and we were going to enjoy life!'

Meanwhile, Ben had put in a search: 'bands, dancing, 2nd World War', and up came a title, 'Let's Dance'. That looked promising. He put the volume up high, clicked on the video and immediately the room was filled with the sound of a dance band in full swing. Hattie's head swung round in astonishment. Ben brought the screen closer.

'That's Benny Goodman!' cried Hattie. 'How that man could make a clarinet sing!'

And now she was shrugging each shoulder up and down in time to the sound of the music. She was loving it!

Ben's mum winked at him. 'Oh, well done, Ben,' she whispered. 'I think this deserves cream doughnuts on the way home.'

***

Later that day, Alex came round. Ben played him the recording.

'Is that Hattie singing! And what's with all the bangs?'

Ben started to explain, then there was a tap on the window. It was Joe. Ben beckoned him in.

'Hey, Joe, do you know this song?'

Joe put his head on one side. 'Think I may have heard it. I've got an app that can identify it.'

'You're joking! Even with a recording like this?'

'It can, I swear. It'll do it no trouble. Play the recording again.'

It didn't take Joe long. 'There you go: it's called "In the Mood".'

Ben was impressed. 'Hey, that's amazing! Her favourite song, perhaps?'

'Yeah, might be. I bet I can find a recording.' Joe started tapping in the title. When the music started it didn't sound like the same song, but then up came the big tune.

'Hey, that's it!' exclaimed Ben. 'Joe, you're a genius!'

'I know,' said Joe, modestly.

CHAPTER 9

Ben was just doing his homework when the phone rang. It was Grandad.

'Ben, lad, I've something to ask you. I'm in the library and I've discovered that in 2008 the ATA pilots got presented with a special badge of thanks from the government.'

'But the war was ages ago!'

'I know. It was long overdue. But does Hattie have a special badge?'

'No,' said Ben slowly, 'I'm pretty sure she doesn't. She doesn't really have any special things that are hers in her room, except the tractor and the Spitfire models that Alex gave her and one of Joe's aeroplane posters. She looks at those a lot.'

'Well, if she doesn't have her badge yet we must certainly make sure that she does get one, before it's too late. It must be possible.'

'But how?' asked Ben.

'Write to her MP, I should think.'

'Oh, Grandad! Are you really going to do that?'

'No, I think that *you* should do it, you and your friends. After all, you are the ones who discovered

that she was a pilot. I'll give you some help, though,
if you need some ...'

To: Mr Peter Richards MP,
House of Commons,
London, SW1A 0AA

Dear Mr Richards,

Hattie Barshot lives in Rowan Nursing
Home in Southampton. We have discovered
that she flew planes with the Air Transport
Auxiliary during the Second World War. We
think she should have had a badge from the
government to thank her. All the other ATA
pilots did.

No-one knew where she was because she
was living abroad, so she did not get one but
we think she should have one now. Please
could you ask the minister about it for us?

Yours sincerely,

Ben Barshot (cousin)
Alex Harrison (friend)
Joe Williams (friend)

PS Please could you do it soon because she
is very old.

From: Peter Richards, MP

Dear Ben, Alex and Joe,

Thank you for telling me that Hattie Barshot has not yet been awarded her Air Transport Auxiliary badge of thanks. I have been in touch with both the Department for Transport and the Ministry of Defence and you are quite right: Hattie should have been awarded a badge, and I shall ensure that this happens.

The other ATA pilots came to London to receive their badges from the then Prime Minister Gordon Brown, but since Hattie is so frail, I will arrange for the badge to be presented to her at her Care Home, probably by someone from the Ministry of Defence, as the ATA and Royal Air Force worked so closely together in the war.

I will write and let you know when I have further news.

Thank you for bringing this important matter to my attention.

Yours sincerely,

Peter Richards, MP

CHAPTER 10

'Ben! Alex!' Joe sprinted through the school gates to catch them up. 'Hattie's going to get her badge in three weeks' time and the Air Cadets Band has been invited to play at the ceremony. AND the bandmaster says that because I know Hattie, he's going to let me play! He says Hattie's a local celebrity. The local press will be there too!'

Alex was impressed. 'That's brilliant, Joe! And it's going to happen in three weeks? That's not long. Dad's been helping me make a much bigger model Spitfire for her, one with a motor. We were thinking perhaps we could fly it at the presentation. I *think* we can just about get it finished in time ...'

Joe was enthusiastic. 'She'd like that, for sure! Hey, this is going to be great!' He gave Alex a high five and then swung round to give one to Ben, but Ben had started to move away.

'Going to be late,' he muttered over his shoulder.

'What's up with him?' asked Joe.

'No idea.'

CHAPTER 11

Ben stared out of the kitchen window. It wasn't raining but he didn't feel like kicking a football about today. Grandad handed him a glass of orange.

'Mum says you've had a letter about Hattie's badge.'

'Yes. Finally.'

'When are they going to present it?'

'In about three weeks – no, it's less than that now.'

'Well, that'll be exciting, won't it? I'm sure you'll be invited.'

Ben nodded dully.

'Do you think your friends will come along too?'

'Joe will be there for sure. He's playing in the Air Cadets Band.'

'Is he, now? I love a good band. And Alex?'

'Think so. He and his dad are working on a model Spitfire with a motor. He's hoping they can fly it at the event.'

'That's ambitious.'

'Yep.'

There was a long silence. Ben returned to the window. His grandad went over and stood beside him. They both watched a fat pigeon land heavily on the bird table, scattering three smaller birds.

'Get off, you great bully!' yelled Ben, angrily. He banged on the window and the bird took off in alarm.

'Ben,' said Grandad, 'Mum took me to see Hattie last week.'

'Yes, I know.'

'You're quite right. She doesn't have many things in her room and the walls are pretty bare. I thought I'd make her a soft board to screw on the wall.'

'Oh. Good.'

Ben continued to stare out into the garden.

'For cards and things, that's what I was thinking … But now I've had a better idea. What if I made a really big, long soft board? You could paint her a sort of mural! Not actually on the wall, but on two or three large sheets of paper that we could pin to the board.'

And suddenly Ben could see it. A long picture, an aerodrome perhaps, with a runway, big hangars and with the pilots and mechanics standing round, and planes in the sky, and one coming in to land …

'Well, what do you think?' asked Grandad.

'It's a great idea, but … how could I do it all in under three weeks?'

'Ah well, that's easy,' replied his grandad, 'you're going to have to recruit some help.'

CHAPTER 12

'A painting!' Joe looked alarmed. 'No. Sorry. Anyway, I've got rehearsals for the band.'

Alex was only slightly more help.

'You are asking me to help you with a proper painting! You must be mad!'

'Please, Alex …'

'Well … I suppose I could help paint the grass or something … Anything more and I'd probably ruin it!' (Which was probably true.)

Ben looked up at the classroom wall. A new picture had been put up. A street scene, filled with people, battling a strong wind. It was so lively and interesting.

Ben quickly looked away. The picture was better, he thought, than anything he had ever done. He turned to check. Yes, there was the signature. Milena. Not that there could be any doubt. She was really talented. He looked at one of his own pictures on the opposite wall. It didn't seem so special now.

***

Ben kept thinking about the long picture he had imagined, but somehow the confidence he had felt before had faded away. By breaktime he had decided.

'I'm not going to do the mural,' he told Alex. 'It would be too difficult and there's not enough time. It was a silly idea.'

Alex was not taken in. 'No, it wasn't! You're brilliant at art – and you *know* who you need to ask to help …'

***

For the rest of that morning, nothing went right for Ben. He made mistakes in his maths, and then got told off for staring out of the window and not paying attention. Trouble was, his mind knew what it wanted to think about and it wasn't maths.

He didn't really know Milena. What would she say if he asked her for help? She might not want to work with him. But then again, if she did, she might be much better than him and think that his work was rubbish. And anyway, what would she say about doing a picture for an old lady that she didn't even know? But he so badly needed help, otherwise it would be impossible. And she might say yes.

Ben's legs felt heavy as he crossed the room, but when he explained his idea to Milena her face lit up.

'Yes, I like very much to help you with this!' And she beamed at him. He began to describe his idea in more detail. Her enthusiasm was infectious. Ben's doubts vanished. Together they could do it, and suddenly he was glad he had asked her for help.

CHAPTER 13

Miss Walker was helpful. Yes, Ben and Milena could work on the mural in their lunch hour as long as they cleared up properly afterwards. And work at it they did, every minute that they could. But at first, things didn't go too well.

'We have to have wartime camouflage for the hangars,' said Ben, 'and the right colours for the planes, of course. But it all looks so dull!'

'Yes, everything the same. Brown and green mostly. Does not look good. I think we start again.'

'But we can't! We have hardly any time!'

'Yes, I know this, but perhaps if we paint airfield looking down from sky …?'

Ben was doubtful. 'Do you really think so?'

'Yes, yes. We try it?'

And she was right. They started again, and looking down there was plenty of variety and colour. A patchwork of fields, green, yellow and brown, the red tiles of houses, blue-green sea gleaming in the distance and the shy airfield tucked away, one plane on the ground, and beside it, a small navy-blue-clad pilot, hair flying, waving at another plane just coming in to land. The painting started to come alive. This was what Hattie had told them about. The joy of it all. The joy of flying.

CHAPTER 14

The day of the presentation arrived, and a carer had taken Hattie to have her hair done. Ben and Milena would just have time to put up their picture, but they'd have to be quick, so Joe and Alex had offered to help.

'You've got the pieces of paper the wrong way round!' insisted Ben. 'That one should be on the right, Joe.'

'No, it … oh, yes, I see what you mean.'

Joe and Alex swopped places.

'OK now?' asked Alex.

Ben stood back. 'Do you think it's straight, Milena?'

'Left side more up, I think … yes, better … That's good now.'

While Joe and Alex held it steady, Ben and Milena quickly put in the pins and then it was done. They all stood back to admire it. It looked good. The swoosh of wheels on carpet told them that they were only just in time. Sure enough, Hattie swept into the room pushed by a carer, but this was a very different Hattie! The ATA had lent her a uniform like the one she would have worn in the war, navy blue, very smart, with a gold wings emblem and two stripes on the shoulder. Her hair had been washed and set and she wore a strange navy-blue cap, pointed at both ends, placed at a jaunty angle on her head. On the left-hand side, the cap was emblazoned with a gleaming, golden badge.

'Hattie,' said Ben, coming towards her, 'you look wonderful!'

The others crowded round, adding their praise. Hattie smiled, bowing her head slowly in gracious acknowledgement of the compliments. Then she caught sight of the painting.

'Oh,' she said, 'oh, what a beautiful thing! It's like my base at Hamble, even that tower over there, like St Andrew's church. A useful marker – as long as you didn't fly into it, of course!'

A sound from outside took Joe to the window. 'The band's setting up. I must go. See you downstairs, Hattie.'

'Oh, am I going downstairs?'

'Yes, for your special presentation.'

And he was gone. Alex went too, to help his dad get the model plane ready.

Hattie looked at the mural again. 'Did you do this?' she asked Ben.

'With Milena. Yes. We painted it together.'

Hattie took their hands.

'How kind of you both. I shall so enjoy looking at this. Thank you,' she said.

CHAPTER 15

A large gazebo had been set up on the lawn, red, white and blue bunting fluttering from the guy ropes. Inside was a table covered in a crisp white cloth. Large vases stood at either end, overflowing with summer flowers.

The residents were grouped outside on the patio, most wearing large, floral sunhats. Other chairs had been grouped nearby for visitors, and evidently the care home was expecting plenty. The band struck up a lively march and all heads turned to listen. Ben could see Joe, seated at the back, his brow furrowed with concentration. He took a quick photo of his friend.

Milena was looking out for her parents.

'I think that is their car … Oh, no … but I hope they are not late.'

Ben had spotted something else.

'Look, Milena – at the white van coming round the corner! It's got a satellite dish on top and aerials. It must be … yes, see on the side … BBC. Hattie's going to be on television!'

'Ben, over there in the car park. Big black car, important people, I think. See, the man just getting out, his ... I don't know word ... special clothes.'

'Uniform. Oh yes! The Air Commodore it must be. The letter said he would be presenting the badge. And those people in the car behind are from the ATA museum. I recognise the chairman. And look, over at the side gate, some of our class with Miss Walker!'

'And there is my parents! Is that your mum and grandfather, Ben?'

***

It was time for the speeches. Ben and Joe wriggled their way to the front of the crowd. The Home Manager clapped her hands to call for silence, and the MP stood up to deliver his speech:

'I am honoured to have this opportunity, on behalf of the government, to offer our sincere thanks to First

Officer Hattie Barshot of the Air Transport Auxiliary for her service to this country in the Second World War ...'

'And about time too!' said Hattie loudly. Everyone laughed.

'Er, yes, you are absolutely right ... Very belated thanks ... These brave men and women of the ATA made an outstanding contribution to the war effort. Flying low, without radio contact, they had to navigate using maps and physical features such as rivers, woodland and railway lines. They risked

their lives to deliver any number of different planes to airfields all over the country ...'

Joe nudged Ben,

'Navigating by eye!' he whispered, 'without radio contact with the ground! *That's* why Hattie was so worried about her pilot friends getting stuck above the clouds in bad weather.'

'... The government would like to show its gratitude by honouring Hattie today. I shall now hand over to retired Air Commodore Sir John Downing to make a special presentation.'

The Air Commodore stood up. A tall, impressive figure in full uniform. He cleared his throat: *'I am delighted to present this badge to you, First Officer Hattie Barshot, in special recognition of your bravery and skill ...'*

Hattie had evidently forgotten that she was getting a special badge and looked very surprised when she was handed the little green box, but when she looked inside her face broke into a huge smile of pleasure. The badge nestling in the silk lining was golden, with a little royal crown on top, a garland of leaves around the sides and *Air Transport Auxiliary* emblazoned in a blue circle. In the centre was a bird in flight. Hattie held the badge up for everyone to see. There were cheers and applause.

Just then came the sound of a little motor, and right on cue, Alex's model Spitfire appeared from behind the bushes. It was much bigger than Ben had expected. The size of a kite, it flew in an arc high above the garden, dipping and rising, weaving around in the air.

Ben glanced over at Hattie. She was looking up, her mouth open in surprised delight. She waved at the little plane, laughing.

Joe went back to join the band and soon they struck up with a lively tune. This time it was one that Ben recognised, Hattie's favourite – and not only Hattie's, it seemed. Lots of the residents were swaying to the music.

Ben glanced around. Tea was being served. Care staff were coming round with plates piled high with sandwiches, little iced cakes, bowls of strawberries and cream and piles of cream-filled meringues. And over at a table, he realised that his mum and grandad were being interviewed by a smartly dressed woman reporter. His mum gestured towards Ben and before he knew it, the reporter was heading his way. Ben's stomach gave a lurch but there was no time to hide.

'I understand that you are a relative of Hattie's too?'

'Yes … that's right. Though we didn't know her until recently.'

'And how did you discover that Hattie had been a pilot?'

Once he started, Ben found he was enjoying himself. There was plenty to tell.

'And what do you think of your famous relative?' asked the reporter, finally.

Ben paused. He thought of Hattie when he had first met her. Just a little old lady. Hattie, who could be crotchety and rude, and who was certainly very forgetful, but who had gradually had so *much* to say. And here she was today, the centre of attention, and very smart in her uniform. Hattie, the Spitfire Girl, who had loved to fly!

He looked at her fondly.

'Surprising,' he declared, '*very* surprising.'

***

Later that evening, Ben sat round the kitchen table with his mum and grandad.

'Wasn't it funny when Hattie's meringue blew off her plate and landed on the grass and she was so cross when the staff insisted on getting her a new one! What was it she said?'

'A peck o' dirt won't hurt!' chuckled Grandad.

'Yes, that's it! And then seeing Hattie watching herself on television! She couldn't quite work it out but I think she was really proud. She'll remember this day for ever now!'

'Well,' replied his mum cautiously, 'she might not, Ben.'

'Might not? She must, she must remember …'

'But her brain doesn't hang on to new memories so well now, does it?'

'Well … no, but surely …'

Grandad put an arm round his shoulder. 'It doesn't matter, lad. The important thing is that she enjoyed herself *today*. She had a wonderful time.'

'I know, but …'

'And didn't I see Joe's dad filming everything?'

'That's true.' Ben brightened up a bit.

'And then there's the beautiful mural that you and Milena painted for her …'

Ben smiled. 'Yes, she really does like that. She keeps pointing it out to the carers.'

Mum winked at him. 'Yes, and not only carers. I saw her beckon in someone else's visitors, to show them her picture! She'll go on and on enjoying your mural, Ben. And what about that special ATA veterans' badge that you helped her to get? She'll always have that to keep and enjoy.'

Ben smiled more broadly.

'Most of all, though,' said Grandad slowly, 'you've helped her remember who she is – for today, at least. And our family and all the care home staff know about her life too, now. You've given her back her identity, Ben, you and your friends. And that's the most special thing of all.'

Ferry Pool 15, Hamble. The Ladies and the Spitfire, 1944.
Photograph courtesy of Maidenhead Heritage Centre

THANKS

I would like to thank all the following people:

My publisher Stephen Chalke and wonderful illustrator Susanna Kendall for their generosity and unstinting support; all those who read drafts of this book and gave me useful feedback; those who have helped me with research, particularly Mr John Webster and the staff at Maidenhead Heritage Centre. Any remaining factual errors are entirely my own.

I would also like to pay tribute to Third Officer Joy Lofthouse, sadly no longer with us, who so kindly shared with me her memories of flying with the ATA.

Last but not least, I would like to thank my family and friends for their encouragement and support, and particularly my brother, Marcus, who has not only given proof reading and editorial feedback and advice but has also been my rock and anchor throughout.

ABOUT THE AUTHOR

Julia Amos lives in the West Country. She has taught instrumental music in schools, and many different courses in creative writing and music in the community. She has also provided therapeutic activities in hospitals, day care centres and care homes. Julia studied Creative Arts in Music and English at Bath Spa University. This is her first children's book.